dedicated to
Mr Peershouse and the
noodle dragon

First published in 2015 by
Macmillan Children's Books,
a division of Macmillan Publishers Limited
20 New Wharf Road, London N1 9RR
Basingstoke and Oxford
Associated companies
throughout the world.
www.panmacmillan.com
ISBN: 978-0-230-75302-0 (HB)
ISBN: 978-0-230-75303-7 (PB)
Text and illustrations copyright
© Ella Burfoot 2015

2 4 6 8 9 7 5 3 1

A CIP catalogue
record for this book
is available from the
British Library.

Printed in China.

Recipe
For a Story

Ella Burfoot

Macmillan
Children's Books

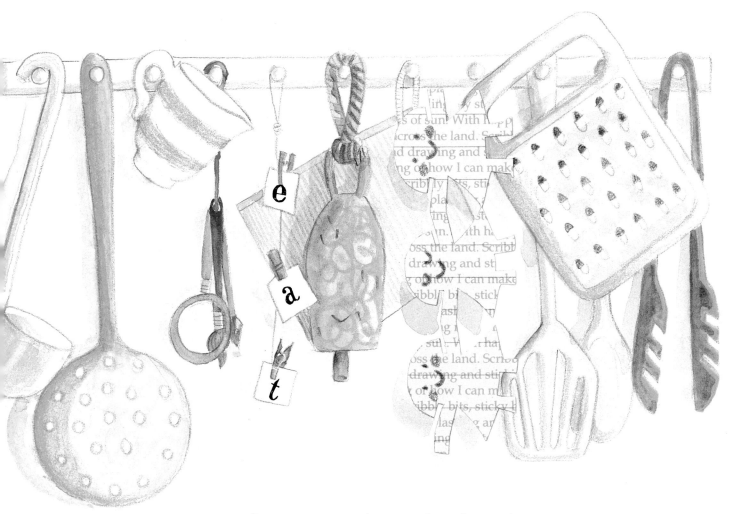

I am going to cook a book!

I'll break some thoughts into a cup.

I'll beat them, whisk them, mix them up.

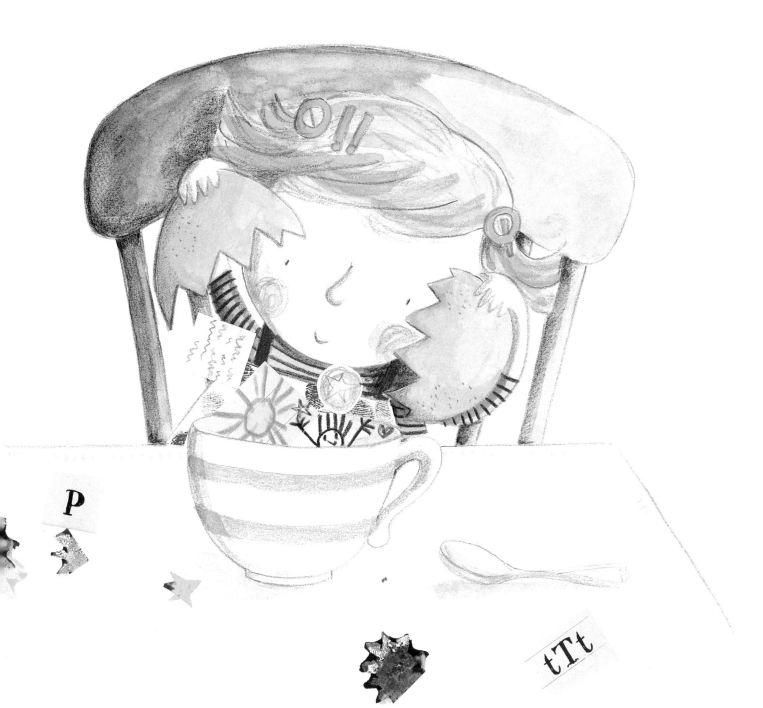

I'll weigh out the
words – just enough.

BIG
WORDS

Small
words

MIXED
WORDS

Choosing the right
ones can be tough!

The small ones go into the pot,

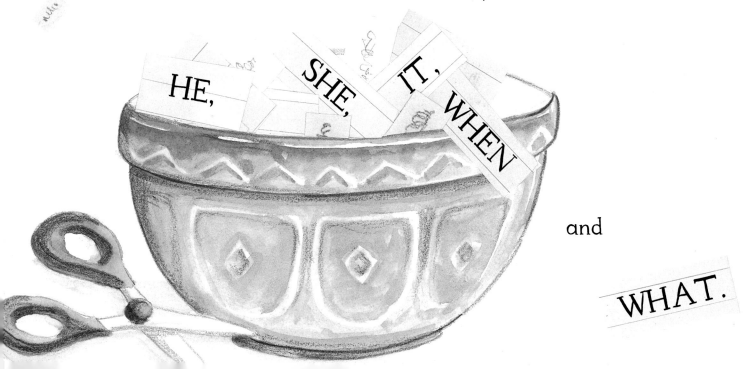

HE,

SHE,

IT,

WHEN

and

WHAT.

I'll drop some big words from a height,

ELEPHANT,

CROCODILE,

DYNAMITE!

COOKING FOR CREATIV

AWFUL AUTHORS AND TERRIB

Fairy Cakes and

TASTY TAL

WOLF IT DOWN   by B.B

GOLDILOCKS

FANTASY
FLANS   and

The Princess ar

ECI

Y CA

Now that my story has begun,

I'll cut out characters, one by one.

Feelings, colours, sounds, a picture
All add flavour to my mixture!

Giggly Word Preserve

ZAP MA WC

Sad Words

I'll add a watery word or two.

I'll pour them in and stir them through.

Splish, splosh, splash, drip or sprinkle.

Glug and gurgle, squelch and tinkle.

Now I'll put a lid on it.

Wait a while.

Let it sit.

It's not until I roll it out
That I'll find out what it's all about!

And now I'll lay it in the tin,

So
my
characters
can
jump
in!

Next, the middle,
   the action, the filling!
Into the pan,
   without any spilling.

Now all I'll do
   is simply add
A spoon of good
   and a pinch of bad.

Turn up the heat –
   let the bubbles quicken.
And then my plot
   begins to thicken.

MONSTER FLAKES

Alphabet Spaghetti

BITTER BEANS

BOWS and FRILLS

SWEET PEAS

Granny's

WOLF

Weet

SLICES OF QUINCE

Full Stop Capital Let[ter] Dried Princess Peas

Every sentence
    will taste much better
If I add a full stop
    and a capital letter.
But where did I put them?
    I've seen them myself . . .
Here they are in the cupboard,
    on the top shelf!

STORY POPS

Porridge Oats

ENORMOUS TURNIP Slices

Lastly the ending – I'll press it down,
And add decoration all around.

I will glaze with happiness,
leave it to cook,

Then bake it, brown it,
and finish my book!

I turn the pages and I can tell

That my recipe's turned out well.

I've done everything that I need . . .

To make my story a delicious read!

Now you have all
the ingredients,
why not cook up a
story of your own?